If I had a pig

MICK INKPEN

WITH CARE

LITTLE BROWN AND COMPANY

Boston · Toronto

First U.S. Edition

First published in Great Britain 1988
by Macmillan Children's Books

Library of Congress Catalog Card No.: 87-24489

Printed in Hong Kong

If I had a pig…

I would tell him...

...a joke.

I would hide from him…

...and jump out. Boo!

We could make a house…

...and have our friends sleep over.

We could paint pictures…

...of each other.

We could have fights...

...and piggybacks.

On his birthday…

...I would bake him a cake.

I would race him...

...to the park.

If it snowed…

...I would make him a snowpig.

We would need our boots...

...if it rained.

We could stay in the bath…

...until we wrinkled up.

I would read him a story…